Following Jesus Through Mark

A Lenten Journey

Joe R. Baskin

Introduction

For many years it has been my desire to prepare my-self for the celebration of Easter by meditating during the days of Lent on the life of Jesus guided by the reading of one of the four gospels. The aim of the following brief guide is to enable the reader to follow the events of Jesus' life as they unfold in our earliest and most basic gospel: Mark. It is hoped that the reading of Mark and the meditations that follow will help the reader to follow Jesus more faithfully today.

This guide divides the sixteen chapters of Mark into forty sections suitable for reading during the days of Lent. One important benefit of the book will be the thoughtful and meditative exposure of our hearts to Jesus as he comes alive through the pages of this Gospel. A few suggestions about the reading of the texts are in order. (1) Before you begin to read take a few minutes to relax and quiet your heart. (2) Seek to place yourself in the scene described in the reading. Note the surroundings, visualize yourself as present. See the sights and colors in your mind's eye. Seek to feel the dynamics of what is going on. (3) Read slowly. Let the words sink into your heart. Let your Spirit-led imagination follow the thoughts that come to you. You are exposing your soul to the life of the One who is the best news ever to come into the world.

Our aim is well expressed by the prayer of Richard of Chichester (1197-1253)

> To see Thee more clearly
> To love Thee more dearly
> And follow Thee more nearly
> Day by day.

Notes:

The readings begin on Ash Wednesday and continue to Easter. There are no readings for Sundays.

At the conclusion of each day's reading a prayer or thought for meditation is offered. You may want to interact with the reading by recording some of your own thoughts which come to you from the reading.

When I have been able from my own experience, I have suggested a hymn or chorus to reinforce the reading and help one carry the thought throughout the day. You may add others from your own experience.

A constant companion in my reading of Mark for these meditations has been the commentary of Robert Stein, Mark (Grand Rapids: Baker, 2008).

Following Jesus Through Mark

A Lenten Journey

Contents

Contents

Day I

The Beginning of the Gospel

Mark 1:1-8

Mark 1:1 initiates the beginning of the Gospel of Mark and the beginning of our journey with Jesus during Lent. Mark begins his gospel with an account of John the Baptizer, who figures in the opening of Jesus' ministry in all of our gospels. John's role makes it clear that the career of Jesus is firmly anchored in the Old Testament and is a continuation/fulfillment of that story. The story of Jesus is of one piece with the acts of God recorded in the Old Testament—the creation of the world and mankind, the call of Abraham to be a blessing to all the peoples on earth, the deliverance of his people from Egyptian bondage, the gifts of the law and of the promised land, the glorious and shameful history of God's wrestling in judgment and grace with his covenant people. The story of the gospel is not just a spiritual deliverance of individual souls from the prison house of the body (dualism); neither is it just a new self understanding (existentialism), nor a discovery that you are really God in the depths of your soul (new age). It is the story of the fulfillment of God's promises to liberate creation from its bondage to sin and bring about the true Kingdom of God on earth. That is the Good News of the biblical salvation which Jesus brings!

John's message is one of repentance for the forgiveness of sins. That is an appropriate place for us to begin our

Lenten journey. Repentance has a place throughout our lives. As James tells us, "God opposes the proud but gives grace to the humble....Draw near to God and he will draw near to you. Cleanse your hands ye sinners and purify your hearts, ye men of double minds" (James 4:6-8).

Ash Wednesday helps us to realize our mortality and our complete dependence upon God for life and breath. As we follow Jesus through Mark we desire to purify our hearts and minds so we may experience a deeper knowledge of Christ.

John the Baptist prepared the way and pointed to the "mightier one who would baptize with the Holy Spirit." Jesus is the One who would bring the power and presence of God to a new level in this life (baptize with the Holy Spirit).

Prayer: Father, cleanse me from sin and strengthen me to follow Jesus.

Day 2

Baptism and Temptation

Mark 1:9-13

Among the multitudes that come out into the barren wilderness of Judea to hear John's fiery preaching and to be baptized by him, confessing their sins, there appears a young carpenter from the north. Nazareth in Galilee, Jesus' hometown, was a village of some 500 inhabitants that is not even mentioned in the Old Testament, Talmud or Josephus. That Jesus should undergo baptism at the hands of John is not problematical for Mark (as it seems to be for Matthew) because he sees it as the fulfillment of John's ministry. The "mightier one" who baptizes with the Holy Spirit has arrived. At his baptism this "mightier one" himself receives an anointing with the Spirit.

The baptism of Jesus receives both a visual and auditory response from heaven. The heavens are "torn apart," and the Holy Spirit descends on Jesus. The only other time Mark uses this verb is to describe the tearing apart of the curtain in the Temple at the crucifixion of Jesus. A new dispensation of the Spirit enters the world through Jesus. The anointing with the Spirit is the essential mark of the Messiah, the anointed one (Isa. 11:2, 61:1). The auditory response is in the form of a voice from heaven addressed to Jesus, "You are my beloved son, in you I am well pleased." What Mark has said about Jesus in verse 1:1 (Jesus Christ the Son of God) is now confirmed by the divine voice from heaven. He is the

Christ, Messiah, anointed one, and he is the Son of God. The figure whose actions we shall follow for the next 38 days is the unique manifestation of the One who inhabits eternity. We who have followed Jesus in baptism have in our own way received the Spirit and the assurance of our adoption into the family of God (1 Cor. 12:13, Gal. 4:6).

The temptation of Jesus in the wilderness does not receive great emphasis in Mark, but we can be sure that temptation by Satan was a part of Jesus' life and will be a reality to all who follow Jesus. Jesus faced the adversary in the solitude of the desert and settled issues that would prevent him from pleasing the Father. He is stronger than Satan, and the angels ministered to him. We can take comfort that the Spirit within us is stronger than the one who is in the world (1 Jn.4:4). To us, too, comes the ministry of angels (Heb. 1:14).

Prayer: Father, thank you that Jesus did not hold himself aloof but identified himself in love with those he came to save. Help me to do likewise. Thank you that the same Spirit that came upon Jesus has come into my life

Meditation hymn: " Breathe on me, Breath of God"

Day 3

The Beginning of Jesus' Ministry

Mark 1:14-20

The summary statement of Mark 1:14-15 sounds the keynote of Jesus' entire ministry—The Kingdom of God. Of course for Jews God was the Eternal Ruler of the entire universe. He always had been, is now, and forever will be the Sovereign Lord. But some things were occurring in their daily experience that were hard to square with the belief that a just and loving God was actually ruling over the affairs of human beings. God's chosen people were being oppressed by Roman occupation and taxation. God's people were subject to injustice, poverty, sickness, and disease and demon possession. They longed for deliverance, for the manifestation of God's righteous rule, for salvation.

Jesus proclaimed that the time of waiting for the salvation promised by the prophets of old was fulfilled. The time of the establishment of God's righteous rule had drawn near. Things were going to be different. One should respond by turning from all sin and believing this good news. How this good news will be accomplished will be detailed in the remainder of Mark's story, but the central claim is clearly set forth here at the beginning of Jesus' ministry. As we read these words near the beginning of Lent we are reminded that nothing less than the salvation of the world is the all-important subject of the events of these days.

The proclamation of Jesus is followed by the unique call to discipleship—"Follow me." Other rabbis had disciples, but they asked the rabbi to allow them to be disciples. Jesus initiates the relationship. Old Testament prophets had called people to follow God's teaching and laws. Jesus said, "Follow me." This following involved sacrifice--they must leave their nets and kin and forsake all. The act of following involves obeying the Master's commands. But there is also a commitment to and a trust in the Person who is followed. Following Jesus involves becoming "fishers of men." We are to be involved in bringing people into the Kingdom of God. By word and deed we are to cast our nets of love and concern around people that our lives touch, praying that they will find the good news of the rule of God in their lives. The call to follow is the most comprehensive and enduring call that comes to one from Jesus. The willingness to follow is the essence of discipleship.

Prayer: Follow, I will follow Thee My Lord, follow every passing day. My tomorrows are all known to thee, thou wilt lead me all the way.

-Howard and Margaret Brown

Meditation Hymn: "Hark the Voice of Jesus Calling"

Day 4

The Mighty Works of Jesus

Mark. 1:21-45

After Jesus calls four fishermen to become his disciples, they all come to Capernaum, a fishing village on the northern shore of the Sea of Galilee which Jesus chose to be the center of his Galilean ministry. It was a town of some 10,000 people whose prosperity was due both to the fishing industry and to the fact that it lay on a major east-west trade route with its local toll station.

Up until this point Jesus had been preaching the good news that the time had come when God was to establish his Kingly Rule, setting his people free from the oppressive powers that held them in bondage. Now Mark shows us Jesus teaching with an astounding authority. This astonishing authority has two features. First, it is different from the teaching style of the scribes who customarily taught the people. The scribe's primary authority derived from the rabbis they quoted, i.e., the sources they cited! Jesus' authority was a personal authority, deriving from his own experience and especially from who he was. Secondly, Jesus' authority is seen in his power to compel obedience from unclean spirits. Because of their superhuman knowledge, they know who Jesus is—the Holy One of God—and must give up their domination of God's creations at the command of Jesus.

Not only demon possession, but also fever, and even the dread disease of leprosy must give way to the powerful and authoritative word of Jesus. He brings the Kingdom, demonstrating by his mighty works the dawning of the liberating rule of God.

Because physical healing and deliverance from demonic forces can easily become the main thing, Jesus had to take measures to prevent this from happening. The healing ministry must not be allowed to eclipse the proclamation of God's coming rule or the soul enriching teaching of its true nature.

Prayer: Lord I thank you that the good news of your Kingdom is not just a message, but a demonstration of power as well. Help me to maintain the balance of word and deed.

Day 5

Power to Forgive Sins

Mark 2:1-12

The mighty works of Jesus described in chapter one are continued in chapter two. Whereas the previous miracles are evidence of the truth of Jesus' proclamation that the Kingdom of God had come near and its powers were already at work in him, the miracle of the healing of the paralytic gives further evidence of who Jesus really is.

Jesus was now so popular that he could no longer publicly enter a city but stayed in unpopulated areas (1:45). He attempted to enter Capernaum quietly but soon the news of his coming got out and he was thronged. Nevertheless, four resourceful people would not be deterred from bringing their paralyzed friend to Jesus , even if it meant tearing up a roof. Jesus' words, upon seeing their faith, seem a bit surprising to us, "My son, your sins are forgiven." These words are probably to be understood in the light of the connection that most Jews in Jesus' day saw between sin and sickness. Whether or not the man's healing was soon to follow without delay we cannot know because the scene is interrupted by the scribes accusing Jesus of blasphemy for claiming to do something only God could do. Jesus' response shows that he is indeed able on earth to forgive sins. Pronouncing forgiveness might be easy, for no one could know if it had actually taken place. But to command a paralyzed man to rise up and walk would immediately make it clear whether a person had real power or not. Jesus succeeded and all were amazed saying, "We never ever saw anything like this."

The demons had confessed that Jesus was the "Holy One of God." Now Jesus' own action in forgiving a man's sins shows us who he is. For who can forgive sins but God alone?

The belief that Jesus is the divine Son of God is, of course, basic to the confession of the church concerning him. His mighty works and his life-story that Mark tells refresh in our minds and confirm in our hearts the true basis upon which the confession rests.

Prayer: We are thankful for the forgiveness that you offer to us, confident that you are faithful and just to forgive our sins and to cleanse us from all unrighteousness." (I Jn. 1:9).

Meditation Hymn: "Grace Greater than our Sin"

Day 6

Jesus and the Tax Collectors

Mark 2:13-22

The scene changes from the crowded house in Capernaum to the seashore where Jesus is teaching another crowd. Concluding his teaching, Jesus walks along the way and encounters a man named Levi (also called Matthew, Matt. 9:9). He was a toll collector, probably on the lucrative trade route (via maris) from Damascus to the Mediterranean port of Caesarea. While not as dishonest as those who contracted with the Romans for a tax district, a practice subject to much corruption, Levi still was an employee of a foreign power and despised by the more religious Jews. Jesus calls Levi to follow him and he leaves his booth and does just that. To celebrate his newfound relationship, Levi throws a banquet to honor Jesus and invites his friends, many tax collectors among them. Jesus, unlike John the Baptist, was able to enjoy a good party, and the guests enjoyed being with him.

Jesus' acceptance of such "sinners," and the merry mood of the party, was too much for the scribes and the Pharisees who had already been offended by Jesus' pronouncing forgiveness on the paralyzed man lowered through the roof by his friends. They do not complain to Jesus, but to his disciples, "Why does he eat with tax collectors and sinners?" Overhearing their remarks Jesus replies with a well known

Greek and Jewish proverb: "It is the sick, not the well who need a doctor."

Jesus' acceptance of the social outcasts is a deliberate action indicating that anyone who would accept the gift could have a part in the coming Kingdom of God. Moral respectability was not a pre-requisite. As we seek to follow Jesus it is a continuing challenge to us to be open and accepting of all people, rather than being self-righteous and judgmental. Tony Compolo's story of his impromptu party for Agnes, the Hawaiian prostitute, catches the spirit of the joyous and celebrative nature of the Kingdom. (The Kingdom of God is a Party. Dallas: Word, 1990).

The celebrative influence of Jesus' presence is emphasized more clearly in the following conversation about fasting by the disciples of Jesus as contrasted to the disciples of John the Baptist and the Pharisees. Jesus' disciples cannot fast in the presence of Jesus any more than the friends of a bridegroom can fast at a wedding party! Jesus' presence is a joyous time because he brings the Kingdom of God which will right the wrongs of the world. The metaphor of the wedding feast is often used in scripture to refer to the arrival of the Kingdom of God (Matt. 22:1-14, 25:1-13, Rev. 19:7-9.) The time of salvation has come!

Prayer: Lord Jesus, fill my heart with the reality of your loving presence so that your joy will overflow like sparkling new wine and attract people to you.

Meditation Hymn: "Rejoice, the Lord is King:"

Day 7

Lord of the Sabbath

Mark 2:23 – 3:6

These two stories both deal with controversies between the Pharisees and Jesus over the Sabbath. It is difficult for us to realize either the importance of the Sabbath to the Jews or the extremes to which the Pharisees had gone to safeguard the "sanctity" of the Sabbath. As to the latter, the Mishna lists 39 classes of "work" that are prohibited on the Sabbath. Sabbath breaking was regarded as a capital offense (Ex. 31:14-15). Dozens of rules had been derived to make clear things prohibited on the Sabbath.

In both of these stories Jesus makes it clear that meeting human need is more important than keeping the minutiae of religious rules. The only occasion that Mark tells us Jesus got angry is when he saw religious leaders more concerned Sabbath rules than about a sick man. Jesus indicates the divine intention of the law by stating, "The Sabbath was made for man and not man for the Sabbath." Furthermore it is observed that, "The Son of Man is Lord of the Sabbath." Jesus has authority over religious institutions. He has new wine that requires new wineskins. Our problem today in regard to Sabbath keeping is the opposite of the Jews of Jesus' day. They took the Sabbath too seriously; we don't take it seriously enough. The Sabbath was made for man. We need it! There is a blessing in a Christian observance of "Sabbath" -- observance in the spirit of Jesus who is the Lord of the

Sabbath. (A helpful book on such a keeping of Sabbath is Marva Dawn, <u>Keeping the Sabbath Wholly</u> (Grand Rapids: Erdmanns, 1989).

Prayer: Thank you Jesus that you are Lord over all religious institutions. Grant me the wisdom and the ability to rightly observe the Sabbath.

Day 8

The Twelve

Mark 3:7-19

In contrast to the opposition of the religious leaders, the response of the common people to Jesus was overwhelming. People came from as far away as Idumea (south of Judea) and Tyre and Sidon (cities north of Galilee). The crowds along the seashore pressed upon Jesus so strongly that he needed to have an "escape hatch," provided by a little boat held in readiness by his disciples. There were scores of healings and exorcisms. As usual the demons recognized Jesus as the Son of God, and when he expelled them he commanded them not to make him known. This so-called "Messianic Secret" is to be understood in part as an attempt to avoid fanning the revolutionary hope among the Jews, thereby causing a confrontation with the Romans. The overarching impression of this story is of the magnetic appeal of Jesus' popularity and his mighty power as a healer. The spirit powers, evil as they are, know Jesus' true identity—He is the Son of God.

In verses 13ff the scene changes from the seaside to an unnamed mountain where Jesus summons twelve men from among his followers to be a special group. The symbolism of twelve indicates that Jesus sees his ministry as a restoration of Israel. He is bringing the long awaited Kingdom of God to Israel. Furthermore, these Twelve will be the guarantors of the Jesus tradition (emphasized especially by Luke). They are eyewitnesses to the events when the Son of God walked the earth, and they received from him the true interpretation of his words and deeds. In another sense they serve as examples *par excellence* of what it means to be a follower of Jesus. Such following has two alternating phases. They are to "be with him" and to be "sent out" on Kingdom mission. They learn from him by being with him. They hear, see and interact. They are subject to his personal impact as well as his instruction. They are also sent out to engage in the same kind of activity—preaching the good news of the Kingdom and casting out demons (which he specifically gives them authority to do). Christian discipleship involves both contemplation and action—being with Jesus to learn from him, be inspired and challenged by him and to undertake the tasks on which he sends us. The goal of these meditations is to facilitate both phases of this discipleship.

Prayer: Open my heart, Lord, to experience your presence. Open my eyes to see the work you would have me do today and strengthen my will to do it.

Meditation Hymn: "Hark the Voice of Jesus Calling"

Day 9

The Misunderstood Jesus

Mark 3:20-35

In these verses we have two groups of people who misunderstand Jesus—his family and the scribes from Jerusalem.

Jesus' family thinks he is "out of his mind." Their reason for thinking so is that Jesus is so busy he does not even have time to take care of his most basic need—to eat. Acting out of concern for his well being, they come and try to seize him and take him home. Jesus' family is not the last family to be concerned that some member's obedience to God was "crazy." How many mission volunteers have heard family say, "You are not going to take my grandchildren to the mission field, are you?" When Jesus' family actually came to get him, Jesus used the occasion to teach that obedience to the will of God takes precedence over all family ties. True brotherhood is more a matter of spirit than of flesh.

The scribes' misunderstanding of Jesus did not arise out of concern for his welfare but opposition to what Jesus was about. They could not deny that Jesus had shown great power in casting out demons, but they attributed it to the god of this world rather than to the God of heaven. They accused him of being in league with Beelzebub, another name for Satan. Jesus said that if that were the case the Kingdom of Satan would self-destruct. Mark tells us that the true reason for the liberating power of Jesus was that he was stronger than Satan.

Jesus had bound Satan and consequently was able to plunder his goods. We can take courage, for Jesus was manifested to destroy the works of the devil (I John 3:8), and he who is within us is greater than he who is in the world (I John 4:4).

The "unpardonable sin," blasphemy against the Holy Spirit, is to be understood as attributing the work of God to the devil, showing that one cannot (or will not) recognize the work of the Spirit of God. Without the Spirit's work repentance and faith are not possible and consequently neither is forgiveness. To think that one has committed an unpardonable sin would be deeply troubling, but if one is concerned about it that is clear evidence that one can still hear and respond to the Spirit.

Prayer: Father, help me to clearly understand Jesus and his work in the world, then and now. Help me to respond to your Spirit's leading today.

Day 10

In Parables

Mark 4:1-34

This chapter is a collection of parables. Mark begins the collection with the account of Jesus teaching beside the sea from his boat pulpit. The parable of the sower/soils was probably delivered there to the crowd. In verse 10 the scene changes to a more selective audience of his followers who ask him about his teaching in parables. After Jesus explains his reason for using parables (see the note below), Mark gives us several other parables that might have been spoken on other occasions, as parable seems to be Jesus' chosen method of teaching. By it he moved from the known to the unknown, the familiar to the unfamiliar, from daily life to the message of the Kingdom of God.

Indeed the secret/mystery of the Kingdom of God is the key to understanding the parables. This secret, which the disciples had been "given" (by God's grace) and which "outsiders" did not possess, is the knowledge that Jesus brings the Kingdom in his own person. It is even now breaking in through his preaching, teaching and healing. Through vivid and enduring images and metaphors the truths of the Kingdom find lodging in our hearts. Our hearts are to be good soil in which the word/seed of the Kingdom produces much fruit. The lamp of the Kingdom message will give light to all. We may not be able to understand its mysterious working but the harvest surely comes. The Kingdom inaugurated by Jesus may be small now but it shall become the greatest of all realities.

Prayer: Father, as I hear again the parables of Jesus I give thanks that it has been given to me to know the secret of the Kingdom—Jesus' true identity. Help me to be good soil.

Note on Mark 4:11-12

Verses 11-12 are some of the most difficult in Mark's gospel, for on the surface they seem to say that Jesus teaches in parables with the express purpose to veil the truth from outsiders to keep them from repenting and being forgiven. No wonder the great NT scholar T. W. Manson could say, "This is simply absurd. If parables had this object or result, that in itself would be the strongest possible argument against making use of them, and would make it impossible to imagine why Jesus should have employed such a way of delivering his teaching." T. W. Manson, Teaching of Jesus, p. 76. (Quoted in A. H. Hultgren, the Parables of Jesus, p. 458.

Many efforts have been made to avoid such a difficult understanding. Stein (pp. 209f) lists seven different suggestions for interpreting the hina (usually translated "in order that") to offer a way out of the problem. The best solution it seems to me is the one chosen by the translators of the RSV, NAB and NIV who translate hina not "in order that" but "so that" and further to understand "so that" to be a short way of saying, "So that the scripture might be fulfilled." (Cf. J. Jeremias, The Parables of Jesus, p. 17).

Jesus would be saying that the fact that the "outsiders" did not understand the deeper meaning of his teaching and respond positively fulfills the scripture of Isaiah 6:9-10. The reason that some hear and do not respond in the right way is humanly not understandable. Moreover, those who do hear and understand and respond in the right way do so only by the grace of God. As A. H. Hultgren says, "Faith is a gift of God...revelation is actually a miraculous event that takes place in a person's life by divine decision, election" (p. 459). This is an unfathomable mystery.

As C. S. Lewis says in his <u>Chronicles of Narnia</u>, "Aslan is not a tame lion."

Day 11

Lord of all Nature

Mark 4:35-41

After teaching from a boat all day, Jesus tells his disciples to pass over to the other side (the eastern shore) of the lake. Accompanied by other boats, they cast off leaving the crowd on the shore. As they sail, clouds begin to gather. Presently a violent storm swoops down on them and the overlapping waves begin to fill the boat. The exhausted teacher is asleep on the cushion under the stern of the boat. The terrified disciples rouse him saying, "Doesn't it matter to you that we are perishing?" Jesus arises and commands the wind and sea, "Hush, be silent!" Jesus asks, "Why were you so scared? Do you not yet have faith?" Their fright turns to awe and they begin asking each other, "Who then is this that the wind and sea obey him?"

The primary purpose of this story is to help us to realize who Jesus really is. He reveals himself in word (as in the teaching of the parables) and in deed. This is the first of a group of miracle stories that effectively show the mighty power of Jesus (stilling of the storm, casting out of demons, healing disease and raising the dead). Mark himself answers again and again the question raised by the disciples, "Who then is this that even the wind and the sea obey him?"

Because of the truth of who Jesus is, this story has been used since ancient times to bring comfort and confidence to disciples tossed and battered by the storms of life.

Katherina von Schiegel's words evoked by this story and set to the bracing music of Jean Sibelius' <u>Finlandia</u> have brought strong comfort to many:

Be still, my soul; the Lord is on your side.
Bear patiently the cross of grief or pain;
Leave to your God to order and provide;
In every change God faithful will remain.
Be still, my soul: your best, your heavenly friend
Through thorny ways leads to a joyful end.

Be still, my soul; your God will undertake
To guide the future, as in ages past.
Your hope, your confidence let nothing shake;
All now mysterious shall be bright at last.
Be still, my soul: the waves and winds still know
The Christ who ruled them while he dwelt below.

Be still, my soul; the hour is hastening on
When we shall be forever with the Lord,
When disappointment, grief, and fear are gone,
Sorrow forgot, Love's purest joys restored.
Be still, my soul: when change and tears are past,
All safe and blessed we shall meet at last.

Prayer: Lord, help me to trust you, no matter how stormy the sea.

Day 12

Lord over the Demonic World

Mark 5:1-20

This story, so strange to our modern ears, confronts us with many unanswered questions. What are demons? Can they really affect man and beast as this story describes? Is exorcism for real? Can demons be drowned? Why would people want a mighty healer to leave their country?

But for the people of Jesus' day (and millions today who live in the developing two-thirds world) the demonic power of evil spirits is a very real part of their experience. Attempting to see this passage through the eyes of Mark and his hearers enables us to see what scripture proclaims in this powerful story.

The demon possessed man is leading a miserable and tortured existence. He must live in isolation among the tombs. He is not only hostile and antisocial, but tormented and self-destructive, cutting himself with stones, crying out night and day. He is totally out of control and can't be restrained even with chains. Mark's explanation is that he is possessed by thousands of demons. (A legion consisted of three or four thousand men). Yet even these powerful demons kneel before Jesus and recognize that he is "the Son of the Most High God" (v. 6-7). They, like the wind and the waves, must obey him and depart at his command leaving the formerly possessed man "seated, clothed and in his right mind" (v. 15). Jesus is Lord even of the demonic powers.

Whatever <u>our</u> belief about demons, we all recognize that there are destructive and enslaving powers beyond our control at work in our world and in people's lives. These powers frequently make life miserable and horrible. But Jesus is Lord! The oppressive powers must yield to his control. The way of the cross, self-giving love in obedience to the Son of the Most High God, will lead to the liberation of God's good, but oppressed, creation (Rom. 8:19-21).

Prayer: Thank you that Jesus is able to deliver us from the demonic forces that can make human life tormented. Help me to be an instrument of your liberating power.

Day 13

Lord over Disease

Mark 5:21-34

Mark's account of the healing of the hemorrhaging woman is sandwiched in between his narration of the healing of Jairus' daughter, which we will consider tomorrow. The condition of the woman is dire. She has been hemorrhaging for twelve long years. She had spent a lot of time and money going to doctors resulting only in a worsening physical condition and complete financial impoverishment. When she heard stories of this young rabbi who healed people, hope began to flicker in her despairing soul. "Maybe he could help me," she thought, so she took measures to seek Jesus out. Hearing that he was again in the region she joined the throng of people who were also seeking Jesus. As she was jostled in the crowd she wondered how she might get Jesus to consider her case. She thought to herself, "If I could only touch his robe I could be healed."

Observe her as she makes her way through the press and touches the hem of his garment. Instantly, healing power flows into her weary body. She is cured! But she is also terrified when Jesus turns and asks, "Who touched me?" Her fear is calmed, however, when Jesus says, "Go in peace. Your faith has made you whole!"

Jesus has power over disease! Not all diseases are healed. Some are. Jesus' healing of this woman is a sign that one day all diseases will be healed (Rev. 21:4). The touch of faith gives hope and help here and now.

Dr. L. Lewis Wall, founder of the Worldwide Fistula Fund, provides a moving present-day application of this story. Pregnancy related fistulas cause hundreds of women in Africa horrible suffering and isolation much worse than that of the hemorrhaging woman in Mark's story. They can be healed by a simple operation which Dr. Wall and his team perform. (See Worldwide Fistula Fund.org).

Prayer: Lord, grant me the faith to reach out and touch you and be made whole. Lead me to aid women today who are suffering a worse fate than even this poor woman.

Day 14

Lord over Death

Mark 5:35-43

Only a parent (or grandparent!) can fully understand the deep anxiety caused by the sickness of a child, especially if the child seems near death. Such anxiety is experienced by peasant and synagogue ruler alike. Jairus, the synagogue ruler, oblivious of any social standing he might have had, falls at Jesus' feet and begs him earnestly to "Come, my child is at the point of death." Jesus immediately sets off to his house, but is hindered by the press of the crowd and the incident of the hemorrhaging woman. After this agonizing delay, messengers arrive saying that the girl is dead so don't trouble the Teacher anymore. Jesus ignores the report and tells Jairus "not to fear but only believe." Accompanied by Jairus and his three closest disciples, Jesus hastily makes his way to Jairus' house, only to find mourners weeping and wailing in near-Eastern fashion for the dead girl. Jesus puts them all out, and taking the father and mother along with the three disciples he enters the room where the girl lies. Taking her hand gently he says in Aramaic, "Talitha, kum—little girl, arise." Immediately she arose and began to walk about. Jesus commanded them to give her something to eat and strictly charged them to tell no one.

Jesus is compassionate towards children. He heals a nobleman's son (Jn. 4:49ff), an epileptic lad (Mk. 9:17-27), a

Syrophoenician woman's daughter (Mk. 7:24-30). He receives children in his arms and blesses them (Mk. 10:13-15). Unfortunately, there are more suffering and exploited children today than there were in Jesus' time. Fortunately, there are scores of organizations devoted to saving the children—such as World Vision, Compassion International, Save the Children and many others. One of the ways we follow Jesus is to become involved in ministering to hurting children.

For Mark, the primary emphasis of this story lies elsewhere. It is that Jesus' power extends beyond sickness even to death itself. He is Lord even here. The powers of the Kingdom of God are already breaking into this age through the mighty works of Jesus. He has power over the "last enemy."

Jesus' word to Jairus in the face of devastating news—your daughter has died—is a word of hope to troubled souls who will believe in Jesus. "Fear not, only believe." No matter what awful news we may face, Jesus still counsels us, "Fear not, only believe." Life's difficulties and tragedies can be overcome if, believing in the goodness and power of God revealed in Jesus, we reach out and touch him and obey his word to us.

Prayer: O Lord, who will one day wipe away all tears, give me the faith and love to dry some tears in this hurting world today.

Meditation Chorus: "Only Believe"

Day 15

A Prophet without Honor

Mark 6:1-6

Jesus' teaching in his own hometown resulted in initial amazement and subsequent rejection. Part of the irony of the whole gospel story is that Jesus "came to his own and his own received him not." In spite of the great popularity that Jesus enjoyed because of his matchless teaching and his powerful works of healing and exorcism there developed strong opposition to him as well (2:7, 15-16, 24; 3:6, 22). Over and over Jesus states that "it is necessary", i.e. part of the divine plan, for him to be rejected and die in Jerusalem (8:31, 9:31, 10:33-34, et al.). We can only marvel at the Divine Love and Wisdom that brought forth such a plan. Furthermore, we can be eternally grateful that God has granted to us eyes to see, ears to hear, and hearts to believe that this carpenter is indeed the Divine Son of God. He is not to us "a prophet without honor," but "a prophet, yes more than a prophet"!

A subsidiary theme in this passage is the relationship of faith to the mighty works of Jesus. More than once Jesus said in Mark's gospel "Thy faith has made thee whole" (10:52, 5:34). In Jesus' hometown the villagers' lack of faith limited his ability to perform miracles. It is certainly wrong to say that if a person does not receive a positive answer to his prayer it is because "he does not have enough faith." Nevertheless, full faith in the power, love and wisdom of Jesus opens us to many wondrous things not possible to those whose outlook is restricted to a modern scientific worldview.

Prayer: Lord, forbid that the mighty works you could do in my community should be hindered by my lack of faith.

Day 16

Mission of the Twelve

Mark 6:7-13

The sending out of the Twelve is a new stage in Jesus' ministry. Previously he had called them to follow him (1:13) and later chosen them "to be with him" and to send them to preach (3:14). Now, after a period of training, he sends them out with the added authority to cast out demons and to heal. Their ministry was an extension of Jesus' ministry. People's response to their message would have significant consequences.

Although the Twelve form a unique and unrepeatable group in the history of salvation, in some sense every Christian bears some similarities to them. We are all called to follow Jesus. We all are to "be with him" and "to be sent by him" to do his work and be his witnesses in the world. In our life mission we are not to be over-encumbered by material comforts, but always trust that our Father shall provide for our needs. We are to be involved in freeing people from the unseen powers that oppress their lives and the sicknesses that afflict them.

We can also be thankful to those who have faithfully transmitted the story of Jesus down through the ages until it reached even to us. Let us pray especially for the missionaries from the two-thirds world who go out with the gospel in much the same manner as the Twelve.

Prayer: Father today we pray for your modern apostles who bear the good news of the Kingdom to those who have not yet heard. We especially pray for the "cricket missionaries" from the developing world who obey your command to go, with so few human resources and financial security.

Meditation Hymn: "O, Zion Haste"

Day 17

A Courageous Prophet

Mark 6:14-29

John the Baptist is traditionally called the forerunner of Jesus. He prepared the way for Jesus' ministry by his fiery preaching which issued in a great revival of turning to God and great expectation of the Coming One who would initiate the messianic age. He also walks the way of suffering and death before Jesus suffers on the cross.

Matthew and Luke add significantly to Mark's two references to John. Luke tells us that John is Jesus' older cousin whose unusual birth was the occasion of a profound prophecy of coming salvation. John grew and became strong in spirit and lived in the desert until the day of his manifestation to Israel (Lk. 1:67-80). When he comes on the scene again he is preaching the nearness of the coming Kingdom of God and the necessity of repentance (with appropriate fruits!) to escape the coming judgment that would separate the wheat from the chaff. All three gospels tell us that when John baptized Jesus, the heavens opened, the Spirit descended, and the heavenly voice approved God's Son. These gospels also mention John's imprisonment and the questions about Jesus which it raised in his mind. Matthew and Luke both record Jesus' high evaluation of John, "Truly I say to you among those born of women there has not arisen anyone greater than John the Baptist" (Matt. 11:11, Lk. 7:28).

Wherein did John's greatness lie? He was completely devoted to God, hungering and thirsting after righteousness, willing to make any sacrifice to be faithful to his calling. He was a courageous preacher/prophet, a man on fire for God. He spoke truth to power and did not mince words. He was faithful even unto death.

Prayer: Lord, help me to be faithful and courageous in living out my calling.

Meditation Hymn: "I Have Decided to Follow Jesus"

Day 18

The Compassionate Jesus

Mark 6:30-44

The mission activity of the disciples was so success-
ful that many people were coming to Jesus for his
healing and teaching. Jesus and his disciples did not even
have a chance to eat. The compassionate Jesus proposed
for his disciples a private retreat for some much needed
rest. Their plans were foiled, however, when some people
noted their departure in the direction of the solitary hills
on the northern shore of the Sea of Galilee. When the
weary disciples and Jesus came to shore the hills were
covered with eager and needy people clamoring for help.
Although exhausted, Jesus was deeply moved with compassion for this leaderless sea of humanity. He began to
"teach them many things."

As evening drew near the disciples suggested to Jesus
that he disperse the crowd so they could go get something
to eat. The compassionate Jesus told the disciples themselves
to give them something to eat; then unfolds the well known
miracle of the feeding of the 5,000 with five loaves and two
small fish.

What is the meaning of it all? One modern pastor suggests that in the command of Jesus for his disciples "to do the
impossible with inadequate resources," we have a challenge
for our seemingly impossible tasks today (and remember that
there were twelve full baskets left over, one for each disciple!).

On a broader level we have here a sign that in the Kingdom of God every hungry mouth will be fed. There shall be no more children with aching stomachs, gaunt eyes, matchstick limbs, distended bellies and orange hair. We, too, who follow Jesus, can raise signs of the coming Kingdom by compassionate work to feed the hungry.

Robert Stein observes that in this story "the arrival of the kingdom is seen in the lost sheep of Israel having received their shepherd (6:34) who feeds them spiritually by teaching them and physically providing food (6:37-44). The Kingdom of God has come, and already the messianic banquet is being tasted" (p. 319).

Prayer: Lord, as we behold the compassionate Christ, may our hearts be moved to help meet the needs of the hungry. May our loving action be a witness to your love and to the coming of your Kingdom.

Meditation Hymn: "Let Your Heart Be Broken"

Day 19

Walking on Water

Mark 6:45-56

Why did Jesus have to compel his disciples to get into a boat and leave after the feeding of the 5,000? John's account enlightens us (Jn. 6:15). The people wanted to force Jesus to become their king! Apparently the disciples were open to that idea as well. Many would-be revolutionaries may have been part of the 5,000. Jesus knows that the way of the sword does not lead to the Kingdom of Peace. Would that his subsequent disciples knew it as well! Jesus himself needed communion with his Father to discern his will and strengthen his obedience.

Jesus' coming to the struggling disciples on a stormy sea walking on the water is an obvious miracle that manifests Jesus as the supernatural "I Am" who is able to rescue and calm their (and our) fears. That they did not recognize who Jesus was in spite of the miracle of the loaves which they had experienced the day before is attributed to their "hearts being hardened." How often do we fail to see the miracle working power of Jesus because of our hardness of heart? Mark mentions this obtuseness of the disciples several times (7:18, 8:21, 9:32, et al.). It is encouraging to realize that in spite of the dullness of perception as well as acts of denial and desertion, Jesus is still able to use them for the furtherance of the gospel.

When Jesus reached the shore the people immediately recognized Jesus and flocked to him for the healing he provided. In this summary statement Mark once again shows us the compassionate power of the One who proclaims and imparts salvation.

Prayer: O Lord, help us to recognize anew the miraculous healing and comforting power of this mighty Son of God. Please come to us over the waves in our times of storm.

Day 20

Clean and Unclean

Mark 7:1-23

This passage clearly shows us that Mark's gospel was written for Gentiles since he goes into great detail to explain the Jewish customs about washing.

The sin of the Pharisees and scribes who criticized Jesus' disciples for eating without ceremoniously washing their hands was that they honored God with their lips while their hearts were far from him, as Isaiah had prophesied. This state of affairs is a danger to religious people even to this very day. Do the words of our lips and our outward actions truly reflect the state and desires of our hearts? Where is my heart? What do I think about most easily? What do I enjoy doing most? Do I truly have a heart for God? Is it my inner-most desire to please him? Are my actions motivated by my love for him? Furthermore, are there traditions in my culture that prevent me from acting in love? Is there anything in my religious tradition that keeps me from hearing and obeying the true word of God?

In this text there is a surprising word of Jesus. He actually abrogates the Old Testament teaching about food laws. These teachings have passed away because their intent has been fulfilled. The preparatory purpose of these laws had done its work. Now in Jesus, who announces the Kingdom's coming, there is no longer a need for these ceremonial laws.

There is also a sobering revelation concerning the nature of the human heart. It is the source of all kinds of defiling activities and actions—evil thoughts, fornication, thefts, murders, adulteries, coveting, deceit, licentiousness, envy, slander, arrogance and folly. This evaluation agrees with the prophetic word of Jeremiah, "The heart is deceitful above all things, and desperately wicked" (Jer. 17:9).

In the light of this truth we are reminded that radical actions are necessary to redeem us human beings–actions like Jesus giving his life as a ransom for many; actions like the regeneration of the human heart; actions like a new covenant where God's laws are written on the heart and sins are forgiven.

Prayer: Create in me a clean heart O God, and renew a right spirit within me. Oh, write your laws on my heart.

Meditation Hymn: "Purer in Heart, O God"

Day 21

A Hard Saying

Mark 7:24-30

This account of Jesus and the Syrophoenician woman immediately raises difficulties for the modern reader. Is it not out of character for Jesus to refer even by implication to any people as "dogs?" Viewing the story in its context may alleviate our difficulty somewhat.

Jesus goes to the Gentile region of Tyre apparently to get some relief from the crowds that were thronging him in Galilee. He needed some time for rest and reflection. He did not want anyone to know his whereabouts, but he could not escape attention. He was so popular and powerful that a woman with a demon possessed daughter came and fell at his feet begging him to heal her child. Here comes the hard word, "Let the children be filled first. It is not right to take the children's bread and throw it to the dogs." The meaning is clear. The "children" are the Jews. The "bread" is the blessing of healing. The "dogs" are the Gentiles. The main teaching is also clear. In the divine ordering, salvation is offered to the Jew first and then to the Gentiles (Rom. 1:16, Acts 13:46). No problem. The problem comes to us from being overly sensitive to the analogy that Jesus uses. The woman was not put off by the analogy. She did not see Jesus' calling her a "dog" as insulting. She could use the analogy too. "Even the dogs eat the crumbs that fall from the table." Jesus had attempted to get some rest from his labor of healing, but he was so impressed by this woman's witty persistence that he instantly healed the child from a distance without even seeing her! What a powerful savior!

Some have seen in this passage an example of the humor of Christ (Elton Trueblood). Jesus is playfully bantering with this woman. She takes up the challenge with her response. Jesus is so pleased with her wit that he grants her request.

Others see a motif of testing here. Jesus' initial reply to the woman's request was to test her faith. Her faith proved strong and persistent and she achieved her desire. We should not be discouraged and give up if our requests are not immediately granted.

Prayer: Thank you, Lord, that your salvation has reached even unto us Gentiles and that your compassion extends to all.

Meditation Hymn: "There's A Wideness in God's Mercy"

Day 22

"Ephphatha, Be Opened"

Mark 7:31-37

Jesus' route described in 7:31 is somewhat unusual, as a glance at a map will show. It is about like saying Jesus departed from Atlanta and came to Macon by way of Gainesville through the middle of Cobb County! Perhaps the reason for such a circuitous route was Jesus' desire for privacy in his movements. In any case he ends up by the Sea of Galilee where a man is brought to him who is stone deaf and tries to speak with great difficulty. Note several things about this healing. Jesus takes the man away from the crowd, puts his fingers in his ears, applies spit (probably on his tongue!), looks to heaven and groans, then commands in Aramaic, "Ephphatha! -Be Opened!" The man is healed, hearing accurately and speaking plainly.

There are some important things indicated by this story. First, Jesus did not seek notoriety. He frequently commands the people he helps not to tell anyone (1:34, 1:44, 3:12). While healing was an important element in the coming of the Kingdom, it was not the only thing. The correct understanding of the nature of the Kingdom and a right relationship with the King were equally, if not more, important. The suffering servant nature of Jesus' understanding of messiahship was much different from popular expectations of a political deliverer. Second, we see that Jesus was such a powerful figure that he could not be hidden, nor were people able to keep silent.

They had to tell what they had seen and heard. Third, their remark that "He has done all things well, he makes the deaf to hear and the dumb to speak" suggests that they see the messianic fulfillment of Isaiah 35:5-6.

> The eyes of the blind shall be opened,
> And the ears of the deaf unstopped
> Then shall the lame man leap like a hart
> And the tongue of the dumb shall sing for joy.

The groaning prayer of Jesus and his command for ears to be opened suggest that this is a continuing need of those who would be his disciples. (Ps. 40:6-8)

> Sacrifice and offering thou dost not desire
> But thou hast given me an open ear.
> Burnt offering and sin offering thou hast not required.
> Then I said, "Lo, I come; in the roll of the book it is written of me:
> I delight to do thy will, O my God;
> Thy law is within my heart."

Prayer: Open my ears, Lord, that I might hear both the deep needs of others and the promptings of your Spirit.

Meditation Hymn: "Open My Eyes That I May See"

Day 23

Do You Still Not Understand?

Mark 8:1-26

Today's reading contains four happenings: (1) The feeding of the 4,000 (2) the Pharisees demanding a sign (3) the conversation about the leaven of the Pharisees and of Herod and (4) the healing of a blind man at Bethsaida. An element found in all of them is a lack of perception.

The feeding of the 4,000 has many parallels with the feeding of the 5,000 in chapter six. They are so much alike that some have suggested that they are two accounts of the same story, but most scholars understand that these were two separate events. The disciples seem to have forgotten what Jesus did for the crowd of 5,000 before, and when he suggests that the crowd be fed they ask, "How is it possible to satisfy them with bread here in this wilderness?" Jesus inquires about their resources and takes the seven loaves and few fish, blesses and breaks them to be distributed by the disciples—and seven large baskets full of leftovers are gathered up.

In the next event some Pharisees, arguing with and testing Jesus, ask for a sign from heaven that would reveal God's approval of Jesus in an irrefutable way. Jesus' mighty works, many of which had been done publically were "sign enough" for anyone whose heart was not hardened to God's influence. Signs were possible to those whose hearts were right, but for "the generation" of the hard-hearted no sign would be given." Signs on demand" are not forthcoming.

As Jesus and his disciples leave by boat from Dalmanutha to Bethsaida, he warns them about "the leaven of the Pharisees and of Herod" i.e. their teachings. Elton Trueblood has interpreted the leaven of the Pharisees as too strict and legalistic, a religion that ignored things such as justice and mercy. Herod's leaven, on the other extreme, was a worldliness that sought comfort and power. Both are to be avoided.

The disciples misunderstand Jesus and think he is taking them to task for not bringing enough bread along with them. In the face of their concern about bread Jesus reminds them of how he had miraculously met their needs and more in the past. He asks, "Do you have hardened hearts? Having eyes do you not see? Having ears do you not hear? Do you not remember? Do you not yet understand?" Do you not yet understand who Jesus is and what he can do? Alas, many of his present day followers "are slow of heart to believe." While praying for more faith, we can take heart that in spite of our spiritual slowness and imperfection Jesus is still able to carry out his Kingdom purposes.

The blind man at Bethsaida has further encouragement for those having difficulty seeing. The two-stage healing graphically shows us that the sight-giving touch of Jesus is needed more than once if we are to see all things clearly.

Prayer: Lord Jesus, help us to remember how you have provided for all our needs over and over again. Help us to see the signs you have given and continue to give to help us know in our souls who you are and to help us continue growing in our knowledge of you.

Day 24

Peter's Confession

Mark 8:27-38

This passage is the central turning point in Mark's gospel—the great watershed. The first half of the gospel has presented Jesus in his general public ministry beginning with his baptism at the hands of John, his temptations in the desert, his proclamation of the Kingdom, his calling of disciples and continuing through his teaching about the Kingdom and his mighty works demonstrating the power of the Kingdom and its coming. Now as he withdraws with his disciples from the throngs of Galilee to the quieter villages of Caesarea Philippi on the southern slopes of Mt. Hermon, he inquires as to the impression he has made on the people who had been exposed to his ministry. The populace had believed him to be some important figure in the expectations of the coming Kingdom (Elijah), or maybe some sort of embodiment of the spirit of the martyred John the Baptist, or at least one like the prophets of old, perhaps the one predicted by Moses (Deut. 18:15-19).

Jesus emphatically and specifically asked his disciples what they had come to believe out of their more intimate association with him. The answer, voiced by Peter, shows that they had gotten it right. Jesus is the long awaited Messiah. But they are not to make him known publically. It was much too dangerous. His life could be cut short by the Romans before he finished his work. Moreover, as the conversation with Peter that follows shows, the populace and even Jesus' disciples have a woefully wrong idea about the kind of Messiah Jesus is going to be. (The suffering servant nature of messiahship and Jesus' conditions for discipleship are still difficult to embrace!) Robert Stein observes, "Those who have no room for sacrificial death, atonement, ransom, and so on in their theology of Jesus are warned by Mark that their understanding is more in tune with Satan and fallen humanity than with God (8:33)", p. 404.

Once Jesus' disciples come to recognize that Jesus is the Messiah, he has the task of teaching them what kind of Messiah he really is. He began, for the first time, to teach them that it was necessary (to carry out the Divine will) for him to be rejected by the leaders of the nation, be killed and to rise again. From this point on the Gospel of Mark focuses on Jesus' going up to Jerusalem where he will confront the leaders with his message and give his life as a ransom for many. He will spend less time with the crowds and more with his disciples, trying to prepare them for the coming days.

It is clear from his call to discipleship in verses 34-38 that following him requires a willingness to share in the dangers and sufferings that divine obedience may require. He makes clear, however, that to hold back ones' self from such obedience is to lose the life that really matters; whereas, to follow him in the way of the cross is to really find "the pearl of great price."

Meditation: "He comes to us as One unknown, without a name, as of old, by the lake-side, He came to those men who knew Him not. He speaks to us the same word: "Follow thou me!" and sets us to the tasks which He has to fulfill in our time. He commands. And to those who obey Him, whether they be wise or simple, He will reveal Himself in the toils, the conflicts, the sufferings which they shall pass through in His fellowship, and as an ineffable mystery, they shall learn in their own experience Who He is."

Albert Schweitzer, The Quest of the Historical Jesus,

New York: Macmillan, 1956, p. 403.

Meditation Hymn: "Jesus Calls Us"

Day 25

The Transfiguration

Mark 9:1-13

The Transfiguration of Jesus must be understood in relation to the events immediately preceding—the correct confession of Peter and his incorrect understanding of the nature of Jesus' messiahship. The connection is made explicit by Mark's chronological reference "after six days." The high mountain is not identified, though most scholars today locate it in the foothills of snow covered Mt. Hermon. The mountain is a place of contact with heavenly beings. The inner circle of Jesus' disciples need a convincing revelation that Jesus is indeed the true Messiah despite his declaration that he must be rejected by the nation, suffer and die. They receive this confirmation by means of the manifestation of Jesus' heavenly glory, the witness of the law (Moses) and the prophets (Elijah)and most of all by the divine voice out of the cloud—"This is my beloved Son, listen to him!" This numinous experience fills the disciples with terrified awe, but leaves them focused on "Jesus only."

The primary purpose of the Transfiguration in Mark is to help these disciples to understand at a deeper level who Jesus is. He is the Son of God and the Son of Man who one day will come "in the glory of his Father with the holy angels" (8:38). These three disciples do not taste death before they see the Kingdom of God come with power in the transfigured Jesus

(9:1). For modern day disciples whose faith may be tested by twenty centuries of the delay of the return of Christ, this event (along with the resurrection) is an encouragement to hold on to the belief in the final manifestation of the sovereign purposes of God. As we withdraw for a private time with Jesus it becomes for us a "holy mount" where we focus on Jesus only and are ourselves in some way transformed more into his likeness (II Cor. 3:18).

Prayer: Father, give us eyes to see who Jesus really is and growing faith that our false expectations may be corrected by a deeper revelation of thyself.

Meditation Chorus: "Open Our Eyes, We Want to See Jesus"

Day 26

I Believe, Help Thou my Unbelief

Mark 9:14-29

When Jesus and the three disciples descend from the mountain top experience of Transfiguration he sees the other disciples surrounded by a large crowd and arguing with some scribes. When the crowd sees Jesus they run up to him and are "utterly amazed." Why? Two possible reasons: (1) They had not seen him before though they had been looking for him, or (2) Jesus' face, like Moses when he descended the mount, still shone with traces of heavenly glory (Ex. 34:29). When Jesus asked what they were arguing about, the anguished father relates how he had brought his demon possessed son to Jesus' disciples for exorcism and they were not able to cast the spirit out. When Jesus asked for the boy to be brought to him, the demon violently convulsed the lad, throwing him on the ground rolling and foaming. When Jesus asked how long he had been subject to such attacks the father said, "From childhood, but if you can do anything have mercy and help us!" Jesus turns the focus back to the boy's father, "If you can! All things are possible to the one who believes." The father's desperate cry is, "I do believe. Help my unbelief!"

How often we find ourselves in the father's shoes. We are up against a heart-wrenching problem. (What could be more heart-wrenching than seeing your child suffering like that and "wasting away"?) We have tried to get help but it has been ineffectual. We wonder if anybody will be able to help us, and we cry out in desperation for help. We are told that "all things are possible for the one who believes," and we struggle between faith and doubt. Casting ourselves on Jesus we cry, "I believe, help my unbelief!" The wonderful thing about this story is that such imperfect faith which casts itself on the mercy of Jesus is sufficient! The son was healed.

Prayer question: Do faith and lack faith sometimes struggle in your heart? Cast yourself on Jesus as you cry for help. "He who comes to me I will not cast out" (Jn. 6:37).

Meditation Chorus: "Only Believe"

Day 27

A Hard Lesson

Mark 9:30-50

For the second time Jesus tells his disciples that he is going to be rejected by men and be killed and then rise after three days. They understand his words but cannot fit the concept into their understanding of things. This is not what they understood the Messiah would do. Their being afraid to ask Jesus about it should remind us that there was a sternness and distance about Jesus that should warn us against an over familiarity with "sweet Jesus."

The disciples' misunderstanding of messiahship is further reflected in their immature arguments about who was going to be the greatest. Their dispute offered an opportunity for Jesus to teach about true greatness—humility and being a servant of all. To serve one who had no status like a child in first century society is the kind of attitude which marks true greatness. To lovingly accept and serve a socially unimportant person is to receive and serve Jesus. We do not have to look far to find such people.

Another mark of Kingdom humility is the ability to affirm the work of others in the name of Jesus who do not follow our particular group. Furthermore, it is a hard lesson to realize how serious it is to cause other followers of Jesus to stumble—better to have a mill stone hung around our necks and be cast into the sea! Radical action is necessary to avoid sinning. Anything is preferable to being cast into hell.

The last three verses of Mark 9 are arranged in a catch-word manner with some word in the sentence reminding of another saying that has the same word. e.g. "fire" (v. 48-49, salt (49-50). The disciples can expect fiery trials that will purify them. To be the salt of the earth they cannot lose their distinctiveness. The disciple is to have a purifying and bracing quality of spirit that leads to peace with his brothers.

Prayer: Lord, help me to be a humble servant—not sugary sweet, but with a wholesome, gracious saltiness.

Meditation Hymn: "Make Me A Servant"

Day 28

Divorce

Mark 10:1-12

Jesus has left Galilee and is on his way to Jerusalem via the pilgrim route of Transjordan to avoid going through Samaria. Great crowds gather to hear him teach. Another prophet, John the Baptist, had been beheaded over the issue of divorce at Herod's fortress Machaerus, not far from where the story of today's reading takes place.

The Pharisees appear with a question to "test" Jesus. Were the Pharisees more interested in getting Jesus in trouble with Herod than true concerns about marriage and divorce? In any case there was much discussion in Jesus' day about valid reasons for divorce. The argument often centered on the meaning of the "something indecent" that Moses had mentioned as a permissible cause of divorce (Deut. 24:1). Rabbi Shamai had interpreted it to mean "sexual unchastity by the wife." His opponent, Rabbi Hillel, interpreted it more liberally to include such things as a wife spoiling her husband's supper or a husband finding someone more attractive than his wife.

Jesus by referring to the Genesis creation story frames the issue in a quite different way. Marriage/divorce should be viewed in the light of the divine intention of the institution of marriage—one man, one woman for life—not in the light of what Moses allowed because of the hardness of men's hearts.

At few points do the teachings of Jesus run so counter to the spirit and customs of our age. Rare is the family, in or out of the church, that has not been touched by divorce. Times have changed; the position of women in society has changed, the expectations of marriage have changed, and the pressures of societal opinion have changed. The concern and expectation of the individual for his/her own happiness and "fulfillment" have changed. What has not changed is the divine intention for marriage grounded as it is in the order of creation. Another unchanging reality is the love of Jesus that can help heal brokenness and bring new life.

Prayer: Help us, O Lord, to hold on to the ideal while dealing compassionately and intelligently with the real.

Day 29

Jesus and the Children

Mark 10:13-16

In today's brief passage we see two things: (1) Jesus wants children to come to him. (2) No one can enter the Kingdom of God without becoming like a little child.

Jesus loved children. He was vexed, indignant, that the disciples would scold the mothers who wanted to bring their children to him. He was not too busy to see the children. He would take children into his arms and bless them. (The word for bless here is an intensified form of the word that is used nowhere else in the New Testament!) Children were weak and vulnerable but trusting and loving. In Jesus' blessing we see his tender care and desire for good for each individual. For mothers nothing is more important or fulfilling as to see their children blessed. Jesus is affirming the goodness of the order of creation by touching some of the springs that lie deepest in the human heart.

Jesus still loves children. Is there anything that breaks the heart of God more than the untold multitudes of children today that are suffering and dying of disease and hunger, those exploited through child slavery, those forced to become boy soldiers, or sold into prostitution, or blown up by the bombs of war? Thank God that there are many organizations today that are devoted to relieving the suffering of children. How can anyone who wants to follow Jesus not become involved in some way in helping the world's suffering children?

Jesus used the occasion of blessing the children as an opportunity for a great teaching—unless one receives the Kingdom of God like a child he will never (no way!) enter into it. What does it mean to receive the Kingdom of God as a child? It means to simply and humbly receive it as a gift. Entrance into the Kingdom does not come by great and heroic deeds, nor by figuring things out, nor by keeping the rules of religion, nor by sacrificial giving, but by humble reception of God's love and grace.

In my hands no price I bring
Simply to thy cross I cling.
                                        –Augustus Toplady

Blessed is the person who continues to have a childlike faith in Jesus and the goodness of his heavenly Father. Matthew records Jesus' saying, "I thank thee, Father, Lord of heaven and earth, that thou hast hidden these things from the wise and understanding and revealed them to babes." (11:25).

Prayer: Father, give me the heart of a child, and a heart for children.

Meditation Song: "Jesus Loves the Little Children"

Day 30

Greatly Astonished!

Mark 10:17-31

There are several astonishing elements in this story of the rich (Mk.10:22) young (Matt. 19:20) ruler (Lk. 18:18). First is that such a man would "run and fall down before Jesus." Picture it! Second, Jesus seems to object to this man calling him "good." This does not indicate that Jesus felt himself to be "un-good," but that he is emphasizing God's absolute goodness, and that all goodness comes from God.

A third surprising (to us) element in the story is that Jesus seems to say that one can have eternal life, enter the Kingdom of God, be saved (all synonymous expressions in this story) by keeping the commandments of the law of Moses. In other places Jesus summarizes these commandments with "Love God with all your heart and love your neighbor as yourself.... This do and you shall live." (Lk. 10:25-28). A humble and sincere effort to live by these commandments makes one aware of his need of the grace and forgiveness of God, his need of a sin offering which God provides.

The rich man had done a good job observing the last half of the Decalogue, but as his love of wealth demonstrated, he had not succeeded in putting God first in his life. His wealth had kept him from that.

It is surprising to realize that this rich man, moral and upright, attractive and loved by Jesus loses his soul because he could not give up his great wealth. It may also seem surprising that Jesus would ask of him "to sell all he had and give to the poor." Would we respond positively to such a demand? The command makes sense to us only when we realize that the man's possessions stood between him and Jesus. It may be something else for us (comfort, prestige, plans), but whatever it is, Jesus demands first place in our lives.

Most astonishing of all was Jesus' word to his disciples, "It is easier for a camel to go through the eye of a needle than for a rich man to be saved." According to their theology, prosperity was a sign of God's favor. If it is impossible for a law-keeping rich man to be saved, then who can be saved?

Jesus' reply makes it clear that being saved, entering into the Kingdom is a miracle of God. To have such a humble and childlike state of heart is humanly impossible for self-centered, prideful creatures like us, but it is granted to those who will repent, believe the good news and follow Jesus.

Finally, it is astonishing to be told that anyone who leaves houses or lands, or brothers or sisters, parents or children for the sake of Jesus and his gospel will receive a hundred times more in this life, as well as receive eternal life in the age to come. We readily understand the part about the age to come; it is the promise for "this age" that may be surprising. But those who have left those things can testify that the hospitality, fellowship and provisions in the family of God show Jesus' words to be true.

Thought to ponder: What am I lacking in my relationship with God and my attempts to follow Jesus?

Meditation Chorus: "Seek Ye First the Kingdom of God"

Day 31

A Ransom for Many

Mark 10:32-45

This is the third time that Jesus foretells his coming rejection and death at Jerusalem. With the thrice repeated prediction Mark wants to make it crystal clear that the upcoming events in Jerusalem are no accident. They are not simply a human tragedy, a miscarriage of justice—though they are that. Jesus' coming death is to be seen at its deepest level as a divine necessity. Already in Mark 8:31 Jesus had said that the Son of Man must suffer many things and be killed for the accomplishment of the divine plan of redemption.

The announcement of Jesus' coming death and resurrection is followed by the request of James and John for the number two and number three positions in the coming Kingdom of glory. Jesus' reply is that they do not know what they are asking. They do not understand the sufferings entailed in following Jesus (despite their confident "We are able"), nor the nature of greatness in the Kingdom. Jesus has dealt with this misunderstanding at least once before (Mk. 9:35), and here he emphasizes that Kingdom greatness is the exact opposite of worldly greatness. Kingdom greatness is greatness of servanthood, a lesson that disciples ancient and modern have difficulty practicing.

The supreme example of servanthood is Jesus himself who "came not to be served but to serve and give his life as a ransom for many." This mention of ransom is the seed of one of the principal ways of understanding the saving work of Jesus. His life of service, culminating in his death on the cross, is the price paid to liberate mankind from bondage to sin and error. We may understand his death in terms of an atoning sacrifice where Jesus substitutes himself for guilty sinners and dies in our place, cleansing us from the burden and guilt of sin. Or we may understand it as the price that Jesus paid through his suffering to bring human beings to a true realization of the horrifying result of human sin and the incredible heart-melting love of God. (These two views are not mutually exclusive.)

In any case, the placement of this text after the third prediction of Jesus' suffering and in the context of Jesus' determined and impassioned going up to Jerusalem provides the key to understanding his coming death. As Mark's mentor expressed it, "Christ died for sins once for all, the righteous for the unrighteous, that he might bring us to God" (I Pe. 3:18).

Prayer: Father, since I have been redeemed by the death of Christ, help me to gratefully and humbly serve you and my fellow man.

Meditation Hymn: "I Gave My Life for Thee"

Day 32

Merciful Son of David

Mark 10:46-52

The pilgrim route from Galilee to Jerusalem normally involved two crossings of the Jordan River—to avoid going through the hostile territory of Samaria. The second crossing from Perea into Judea would take place near Jericho, the last city to be encountered before the final seventeen mile ascent to Jerusalem. This sub-tropical city was a favorite place for winter palaces (Herod the Great had built three there!).

As Jesus and his disciples passed through they were accompanied by a large crowd of the curious as well as fellow pilgrims. Mark rivets our attention on one person—a blind beggar sitting by the roadside hoping that pilgrims would be kind hearted. But news reached his ears that caused him to hope for more. Jesus of Nazareth was passing by! News of Jesus' mighty healing miracles had preceded him. When the son of Timaeus heard that the son of David was passing by he threw off all caution and began to cry out loudly, "Jesus, son of David, have mercy on me!" Annoyed, the crowd tried to shush him, but he only cried out louder. The compassionate Christ stopped and called for him. The scoldings of the crowd turn to encouraging words, "Take heart, he is calling for you!" The blind beggar sprang up and stumbled toward Jesus, arms flailing. The kind voice of Jesus asked, "What do you want me to do for you?" The hopeful voice of the beggar replied,

"Master, that I may receive my sight." Jesus answers, "Go your way. Your faith has saved you!" Immediately he received his sight and began to follow Jesus in the way.

This last healing miracle of Jesus recorded in Mark's gospel emphasizes two things: (1) Jesus is the son of David, the long expected Messiah. In Mark's gospel Jesus is the son of David, but he is more—he is the Son of God. Davidic titles are not sufficient to indicate who Jesus is (Mk. 12:35-37). (2) Bartimaeus is an example of discipleship. When one realizes who Jesus really is and receives salvation, the only thing one desires to do is to "follow him in the way."

Prayer: Lord, open my eyes afresh to see the merciful and compassionate Christ and help me to follow him in the way.

Meditation Song: "Then Jesus Came"

Day 33

The Triumphal Entry

Mark 11:1-11

Mark's story of Jesus enters its final chapter when Jesus makes his "Triumphal" entry into Jerusalem. All of his preaching, teaching and healing reach their climax as Jesus confronts the nation's center of power with his message. The time of messianic secrecy is over. His "hour" has come, to use Johnanine terminology. Through humble service Jesus had demonstrated over and over again what kind of Messiah he would be. Now he comes to the time and place where he will give his life as a ransom for many.

During Passover week thousands of pilgrims came to the holy city to commemorate the liberation of their nation from Egyptian bondage. In Jesus' entry into Jerusalem one greater than Moses had come to liberate God's people from the bondage of sin and death. The true Passover lamb is about to be slain.

Though we call it the Triumphal entry, it is a strange kind of triumph. Marcus Borg and John D. Crossan in their book, The Last Week: A Day-by-Day Account of Jesus' Final Week in Jerusalem, imagine "not one, but two political processions entering Jerusalem that ... morning of the spring of AD 30. In a bold parody of imperial politics, King Jesus descended the Mount of Olives into Jerusalem from the east in fulfillment of Zechariah's ancient prophecy: "Look, your king is coming to you, gentle and riding on a donkey, on a colt, the foal of a donkey" (Matt. 21:5 = Zech. 9:9). From the west, the Roman governor Pilate entered Jerusalem with all the pomp of state power. Pilate's brigades showcased Rome's military might, power and glory. Jesus' triumphal entry, by stark contrast, was an anti-imperial and anti-triumphal "counter-procession" of peasants that proclaimed an alternate and subversive community that for three years he had called "The kingdom of God." (Quoted from Dan Clendenin, The Journey with Jesus. net, March 30, 2009.) It is through this community of those with humble, childlike faith who are willing to follow their Lord in the way of the cross that the true future of the world's liberation lies.

Mark will guide us through these momentous events of Jesus' final days when the Son of Man, through courageous, faithful action and unfathomable suffering carries out the will of his Father for the salvation of humankind.

Prayer: Lord, deliver me from the false hopes of worldly political power. Enable me to walk with Jesus through his final days that I might have a deeper appreciation of the costliness of my redemption.

Meditation Hymn: "Hosannas, Loud Hosannas!"

Day 34

The Cleansing of the Temple

Mark 11:12-26

On the day before, Jesus had entered the temple complex and observed its activities. Today he sets out for a decisive and symbolic act concerning the temple. The primary meaning of this event is indicated by the framing of the temple cleansing with the acted parable of the fruitless fig tree. This tree, representing the nation of Israel (Jer. 8:13, Hos. 9:10, 16-17), has leaves but no fruit. Jesus pronounces a curse upon it and by the next day it is withered up from its roots.

The temple was the very center of Jewish life. It had been conceived by David and later built by Solomon in all his glory. This temple had been destroyed by the Babylonians and rebuilt by post-exilic Jews under Zerubbabel. It had recently been extensively remodeled by Herod the Great and was one of the most magnificent structures in the ancient world. Jesus' cleansing of the temple was a symbol of God's judgment on the nation.

The violent actions by Jesus of overturning the tables of the money changers and the seats of those selling doves might seem shocking to us, but it is an indication of the outrage of Jesus at the crass desecration of the holy, both by dishonest dealings and lack of respect for the sacred precincts of the temple. His quotation from the Old Testament is particularly relevant when we realize that the operation had been set up in the Court of the Gentiles. God's purpose for the temple was to be a house of prayer for <u>all nations.</u>

As we meditate on the cleansing of the temple we naturally look in two directions: (1) the organized church of our day and (2) our own lives as temples of the Holy Spirit. Have we as a church failed to produce the fruits which God expects from his people—justice and compassionate service? Are there things in my inner temple that need cleansing? Don Clendenin comments on this episode as follows: "I read the cleansing of the temple as a stark warning against any and every false security, misplaced allegiance, religious presumption, paltry excuses, any self-satisfied spiritual complacency, nationalistic zeal, potential idolatry and economic greed in the name of God..."(<u>JourneywithJesus.com</u>, Mar. 9, 2009).

Prayer: Search me, O God and know my heart
        Try me and know my thoughts
        And see if there be any wicked way in me.

Meditation Hymn: "Search Me, O God"

Day 35

Teaching in the Temple

Mark 11:27-12:44

This teaching is presented mainly in the form of controversies arising out of peoples' hostile questioning of Jesus. The Jewish religious leaders challenge Jesus' authority to interrupt temple worship. Others seek to trap Jesus with a question about the rightness of paying tax to a foreign government. The Sadducees sought to put an unanswerable question to him about the resurrection of the dead. They did not believe in the resurrection. One sincere scribe has a meeting of the minds with Jesus about the greatest commandment and the nature of true religion. Jesus ends all the controversies by showing that "Son of David" is not an adequate term to fully understand the Messiah.

The chapter concludes with biting words about people who seek status and make a show of being religious but mistreat the poor and vulnerable. Finally a poor widow, who gave only two cents to the temple treasury, is shown to have given more than all the rich who from their abundance put in much.

Jesus not only shows himself to be one who can best his opponents in an argument, but he also uses the controversies as an occasion to teach important and profound truth.

These controversies bring to a head the opposition to Jesus that has been building since the early days of his ministry (Mk.2-3). The parable of the wicked tenants (Mk. 12:1-12) powerfully portrays the failure of the religious leaders to please God and the consequent judgment. They understand Jesus' accusation and seek all the more to dispose of him.

Meditation question: How does the church today need to change in order to avoid a failure similar to that of Israel to bring forth fruits unto the kingdom? How do I need to change?

Day 36

Jesus and the Future

Mark 13

As Jesus exits the temple for the last time, one of his disciples comments on the beauty and wonder of the temple, one of the most magnificent structures of the ancient world. The comment provoked Jesus' prediction of the utter destruction of the temple. When Jesus and his disciples had crossed the Kidron Valley and climbed the Mt. of Olives overlooking the temple, four of his perplexed disciples asked him when it was going to happen, and what would be the sign when "all these things would be accomplished."

The remainder of the chapter gives us Jesus' most extensive teachings about the future. Some have wanted to see these words directed almost exclusively to the destruction of Jerusalem, but Jesus also speaks of the coming of the Son of Man in clouds with great power and glory, most naturally understood as the end of the age. While there are many interpretative problems and unanswered questions in this chapter, some general truths are apparent and fruitful for our meditation on this day of Holy Week.

First, the future of the world is not characterized by unending progress. Things are not going to get better and better until the Kingdom of God comes on earth. Rather there will be struggle, suffering and persecution as history unfolds. This does not mean that we cease striving for a better, more just and peaceful world; after all, the role of the Servant Messiah of Isaiah 42:1-4 is to bring forth justice. " He will not fail or be discouraged till he has established justice in the earth" (v. 4). But we know that we cannot do it in our own strength. We can by works of justice and love raise some signs of the coming Kingdom, but he must bring the Kingdom.

Second, this chapter reminds us that Christ knows the way of the future. History is ultimately in God's hands, and it unfolds according to his direction and will climax with the return of the victorious Son of Man. The immediate future for Jesus is one of terrible suffering as he walks the way of the cross, but ultimately the Son of Man will come on the clouds with glory and power.

Third, we are to be busy with the preaching the gospel (in word and deed) to all nations (13:10), even in the face of persecution. We are to be watchful against the powers of evil that would lull us into spiritual slumber amid the comforts and distractions of this evil age.

Prayer: God of grace and God of glory,

Give us wisdom,

Give us courage

For the facing of this hour.

H. E. Fosdick

Day 37

Extravagant Love

Mark 14:1-11

It is Wednesday of Holy Week, two days before the crucifixion of Jesus. The religious authorities are trying to figure out some way to arrest Jesus without igniting a riot during the volatile time of Passover. Mark's explanation of how they are able to do so involves a dinner scene in Bethany, where Jesus is spending the nights of Passover Week.

Simon the leper, in whose home the dinner takes place, is obviously one who had been healed from the dread disease, since he would have been isolated if he were still infected. A woman, unnamed by Mark, comes to the reclining Jesus and breaks an alabaster vial of costly perfume and empties the contents on the head of Jesus. For her, it is an act of extravagant love. The perfume was valued at a year's wages, but she poured it all on him and broke the beautiful container, expressing her overflowing, complete devotion. The fragrance filled the room.

The woman's actions evoked two very different responses—the harsh criticism of "some," and the praise of Jesus. The "some" are probably from the ranks of the disciples, one of whom went directly to the chief priests with information of where they could find Jesus without crowds around him. Their criticism was directed to the "waste" of a year's wages that could have been used for the poor. In Jesus' initial defense of the woman, he notes there are continuing opportunities and unique opportunities. The outpouring of her extravagant love at this unique opportunity is not to be condemned. Jesus' defense of her moves to praise, as he gives a larger context for her action. The woman was expressing her great love for Jesus. Jesus speaks of a deeper meaning. She has anointed his body for burial ahead of time, and she will be memorialized in the telling of the story wherever the gospel is preached.

Prayer: Father, in light of your incredible love for me, I would pour out my heart and life in love for you.

Meditation Hymn: "My Jesus I Love Thee"

Day 38

Maundy Thursday

Mark 14:12-52

As we relive the events of this Thursday of Holy Week, let us envision the two disciples going into the city to meet the man (unknown to them) with whom Jesus had made arrangements to use his guest room for his celebration of the Passover with his disciples. Let us imagine ourselves gathering at dusk with the Twelve and seeing them reclining on couches around the low table laden with the roasted lamb, unleavened bread, the fruit puree (*haroseth*), bitter herbs and cups of wine. Let us listen as Jesus rehearses the story of the first Passover pointing out the significance of each element. Feel the tension in the air as Jesus announces that one of them will betray him and all, one by one, protest innocence.

The most important happening at this meal, however, is when Jesus takes the bread and the cup and indicates that they are his body and blood which are given to seal the new covenant foretold by Jeremiah (31:31-44) featuring the forgiveness of sins and a new heart which desires to obey God. Despite the terrible impending suffering, there will come a new day when the messianic banquet of the Kingdom of God fully comes.

The Passover meal concluded, Jesus and his disciples make their way in the darkness from the upper room up the Kidron Valley to the Garden of Gethsemane where he had often gone with them. Here where the great stones had often pressed and crushed olives to olive oil (Gethsemane = oil press), Jesus would come to terms with the most crushing experience of his life. Jesus desires that his disciples help prepare for the excruciating experience of the coming day. He asks the three disciples who are best qualified to share the burden of his heart to come deeper into the olive grove while the other eight wait near the gate.

Mark's description of Jesus is a bit shocking. The one who had faced Satan alone in the wilderness, healed lepers, cast out demons, raised the dead and stilled the raging sea with his "Peace: Be Still" is "deeply distressed and troubled." We would say he was deeply disturbed and emotionally distraught. He says, "My soul is extremely sorrowful even unto death," meaning "This experience is about to kill me." It was not just the fear of physical pain that he knew was coming, but the coming weight of the world's sins, and the break of his fellowship with his Father that would come the next day when he would cry, "My God, my God, why hast thou forsaken me?" Jesus was facing the hour of his passion, the cup of suffering for the sins of the world. He had to do it alone. His closest friends utterly failed him. They could not watch and pray for one hour!

Jesus' request to his Dear Father (<u>Abba</u>, the only time in Mark where Jesus uses this intimate term to address God) was the essence of faith and faithfulness. He believed that God could do all things. He expressed his heartfelt desire, but ultimately submitted his desire to the will of the Father. Here he finds strength and grace to face the future, no matter what comes.

So when Judas and the soldiers come to arrest Jesus and initiate the events that will reach their climax at the cross, he goes forth to meet them. "It is not a weak, effeminate Jesus of much Christian art who goes out to meet his enemies, but the conquering Son of Man/Son of God! It is the one who is Lord of nature (4:35-41), of the demons (5:1-20), of disease (5:24b-34), and of death (5:21-24a, 35-43). Yet he defeats his enemies by dying for them!" (Stein, p. 665).

Prayer: Lord, I cannot thank you enough for what you did for me. Help me to watch and pray that I may be a faithful follower.

Meditation Hymn: "Go to Dark Gethsemane"

Day 39

Good Friday

Mark 14:53-15:47

O n this Good Friday our time should be spent reliving in our imagination the events described by Mark. We need to expose our minds and hearts afresh to this story which conveys the climax of Jesus' saving work—his giving his life as a ransom for many. The story itself which conveys the historic events is primary. We need to let it have its effect on our souls.

An awareness of the time frame of the various sections of Mark will be helpful as we follow the events of this crucial day.

14:43-72 – Early morning
15:1-32 – Mid-morning
15:33-41 – Noon till three p.m.
15:42-47 – Evening

After exposing ourselves to the story we might find that the great hymns of the cross have a deeper and more powerful meaning for us—hymns like "O Sacred Head Now Wounded,""When I Survey the Wondrous Cross," or "There is a Green Hill Far Away."

There is a green hill far away without a city wall
Where the dear Lord was crucified who died to save us all.

We may not know, we cannot tell what pains he had to bear
But we believe it was for us he hung and suffered there.

He died that we might be forgiven; he died to make us good
That we might go at last to heaven, saved by his precious blood.

There was no other good enough to pay the price of sin
He only could unlock the gate of heaven and let us in.

Chorus:
Oh dearly, dearly has he loved, and we must love him too.
And trust in his redeeming blood, and try his work to do.

Cecil F. Alexander

Prayer: Touch my heart, O God, at the very core of my being and help me to love you as you deserve to be loved.

Holy Saturday

M ark's story of Jesus is completely silent concerning the events of the Sabbath between Good Friday and Easter Sunday. Although this Saturday is the 40th day of Lent, it is suggested that the reader of these meditations save the 40th day's readings until Sunday morning.

Instead of reading the story of the resurrection it would be appropriate to read two Old Testament scriptures which were important for Mark's portrayal of Jesus' death—Psalm 22 and Isaiah 53. This is a day of quiet for the reality of Jesus' death to sink into our minds.

One might also prepare for the reading of Mark's resurrection account by giving some attention to the textual problems in Mark 16. Our best manuscripts all end at verse eight, "for they were afraid." That this seems unsatisfactory is indicated by the fact that the writers of at least two other ancient copies of Mark felt a need to supply a suitable ending to the gospel (often presented in footnote form in modern translations). More importantly, it is evident that Mark himself contemplated a post resurrection meeting of Jesus with his disciples in Galilee (Mk. 14: 28 & 16:7). It is possible that Mark provided such an ending which was lost at an early stage of the transmission of his gospel. However, it is also possible that Mark intended to conclude his story with v.8, noting the fear of some followers among the readers of his gospel to speak of the resurrection of Jesus.

Day 40

Resurrection

Mark 16:1-8

After the sundown that ended the Sabbath, three of Jesus' devoted women followers had bought some spices with which to anoint the body of Jesus, as soon as there was enough light the next morning to do so. Sunrise finds them at the tomb to perform the act of love and respect. They certainly were not expecting any resurrection. Surprised to see the large stone rolled away, they enter the tomb and are terrified from seeing a young man in white (an angel). He knows why they have come: "You are seeking Jesus of Nazareth who was crucified. He is risen, he is not here." They are to go tell his disciples and Peter (what an act of mercy!) that he will meet them in Galilee, just as he had said.

The heart of Mark's account is this angelic word, "He is risen!" The tomb is empty. They can see the place where his dead body was laid a few hours before. The resurrection of Jesus is certainly not to be separated from his remarkable life recounted in the first fifteen chapters of Mark, but it clearly is the crowning event that gives it all its deepest and most glorious meaning. The wonderful good news of the coming/presence of the Kingdom of God had been threatened and almost destroyed by the seemingly tragic events of the last few days. The three women shared the disappointment voiced by the pair on the road to Emmaus, "We had hoped …" (Lk. 24:21). The fact that he is risen brings back the sunrise to their darkest night. It is true after all! Jesus really is the Son of God who has given his life as a ransom for many, who has conquered the last enemy, who has abolished death and brought life and immortality to light through the gospel (2 Tim. 1:10). Mark had begun his book with the "beginning of the good news of Jesus Christ, the Son of God" (1:1) and now he ends his account with the best news of the ages, "He is risen!" He is risen indeed!

HALLELUJAH!

Celebration Hymns: "Christ the Lord is Risen Today"

"He is Lord"

Acknowledgements

The author wishes to express appreciation to the following people who used a draft of the manuscript for personal meditation during Lent and made valuable suggestions: Jan Hardeman, Ruford and Jo Hodges, Carey and Denise Huddlestun, Derek Neal (who read it together with his 11 year old daughter, Emily), Mary Jolley, Steve and Juanita Cordle, Miriam Peterson, Robyn Miller, and Chris Baskin. Helen Ruchti made some helpful stylistic suggestions for a portion of the text. Heartfelt thanks is expressed to Nina Lovel who cheerfully lent her invaluable computer skills to the formatting of the material for publication. I also extend appreciation to Bill Davies for kindly providing the photo for the back cover of the book. Sincere thanks go to my wife Ann who has been a constant source of help and encouragement as she interacted with the text and turned my frequently illegible writing into clear and legible form.

I realize something of the debt I owe to the Christian community, ancient and modern, who transmitted the story of Jesus to me. It is my prayer that this work will be helpful to some fellow followers of our Lord.

About the Author

Joseph Robinson Baskin was born in Alabama and received his higher education at Howard College (B.A., 1951), Southern Baptist Theological Seminary (B.D., 1959) and Princeton Theological Seminary (Ph.D ,1966). He has served as pastor of churches in Alabama, Kentucky, New Jersey, and Georgia. After teaching twenty-two years at Shorter College in Rome, Georgia, he served for ten years as Lecturer at Malaysia Baptist Theological Seminary, Penang, Malaysia.

He is happily married to Ann Fox Baskin, his life-long friend, companion and co-laborer. They have two children and six grandchildren. He is now retired and lives in Rome where he enjoys gardening, fishing, teaching Sunday school, volunteering, and being a grandfather.

6773659R0

Made in the USA
Charleston, SC
06 December 2010